The Three Little Pigs

Grosset & Dunlap

For Adrienne Scott

Grosset & Dunlap

Copyright © 1989 by James Marshall. All rights reserved. Published in 2000 by Grosset & Dunlap, a division of Penguin Putnam Books for Young Readers, New York. Originally published in hardcover by Dial Books for Young Readers. GROSSET & DUNLAP is a trademark of Penguin Putnam Inc. Published simultaneously in Canada. Printed in the U.S.A.

Library of Congress Cataloging-in-Publication Data

Marshall, James, 1942—
   The three little pigs / retold and illustrated by James Marshall.
     p. cm. — (Reading railroad books)
   Summary: Retells the familiar tale in which one of three brother pigs survives a wolf's attacks by using his head and planning well.
   ISBN 0-448-42288-3
    [1. Folklore. 2. Pigs—Folklore.] I. Three little pigs. English. II. Title. III. Series.

PZ8. 1 .M3554 TH 2000
398.24´529633—dc21
[E]

00-057805

ISBN 0-448-42288-3   FGHIJ

Retold and illustrated by James Marshall

Once upon a time
an old sow sent her three little pigs
out into the world to seek their fortune.
"Now be sure to write," she said.
"And remember that I love you."

The first little pig met a man
with a load of straw.
"I know," said the little pig.
"I'll buy your straw and build a house."
"That's not a good idea," said the man.

"Mind your own business, thank you,"
said the little pig.
And he bought the straw and set about
building a house.
It took him no time at all.

Very soon a lean and hungry wolf happened by.
Pig was just about his favorite food in the world.
So he knocked on the door and said,
"Little pig, little pig, let me come in."
To which the little pig replied,
"No, no, no, not by the hair
of my chinny chin chin."

This annoyed the wolf to no end, and he said,
"Then I'll huff and I'll puff and I'll blow your house in."
"Go right ahead," said the little pig.
So the wolf huffed and he puffed
and he blew the house in.

And he gobbled up
the little pig.

The second little pig met a man
with a load of sticks.
"I've got it," said the little pig.
"I'll buy those sticks and build a house."
"I'd think twice about that," said the man.

"Oh, pooh," said the little pig.
"What would you know?"
And he bought the sticks
and went to work building a house.
"Very pretty," he said.

No sooner had the little pig settled into
his pretty house than the wolf happened by.
He was still hungry, and he said,
"Little pig, little pig, let me come in."
To which the little pig replied,
"No, no, no, not by the hair of my chinny chin chin."

The wolf didn't care for that at all.
And he said, "I'll huff and I'll puff
and I'll blow your house in."
"Ha, ha, ha," said the little pig.
So the wolf huffed and he puffed
and he blew the house in.

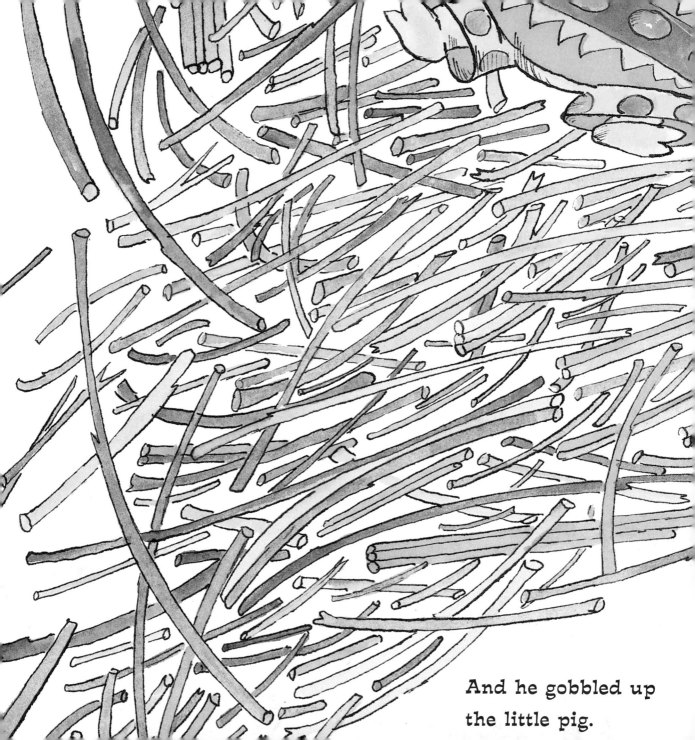

And he gobbled up
the little pig.

Now the third little pig met a man
with a load of bricks.
"These bricks will make a fine,
sturdy house," said the man.
"Capital idea, my good fellow!"
said the little pig.

So he bought the bricks and set about
building a house.
It took him quite a bit of time,
but it was well worth it.
"Nice and solid," said the little pig.
"Nice and solid."

But no sooner had the little pig moved in
than he noticed the wolf loitering about.
And the wolf, who was *still* hungry, said,
"Little pig, little pig, let me come in."
To which the little pig replied,
"No, no, no, not by the hair of my chinny chin chin."

Well, the wolf had heard *that* before.
And he said, "Then I'll huff and I'll puff
and I'll blow your house in."
"Oh, don't do that!" said the little pig.
But the wolf huffed and he puffed
and he huffed and he puffed
until he was quite blue in the face.
The house stood firm.
"I'll try another approach," muttered the wolf.

And he put on his most dazzling smile.

"Little pig, I was only teasing," he said.

"By the way, I hear tell that
Farmer Jones has the most scrumptious turnips.
Shall we go pick a few?"

"Oh, I'm much too busy now," said the little pig.

"What about tomorrow morning?"

"Excellent," said the wolf.

"I'll come for you at six."

The next morning the little pig got up at five,
hurried off to Farmer Jones's turnip field,
picked a basketful of scrumptious turnips,
and dashed back home.
When the wolf arrived at six,
the turnips were already boiling in the pot.
"Sorry I couldn't wait," said the little pig.
The wolf tried not to show his displeasure.

"No harm done," he said.

"By the way, there is a lovely apple tree
down in Merry Meadow.

Shall we go help ourselves to a few apples?"

"I must cook my turnips," said the little pig.

"Let's meet there tomorrow morning."

"Splendid," said the wolf.

"Shall we say at five?"

The next morning the little pig was up at four
and went off for the apples.
It took longer than he'd expected to reach Merry Meadow.
And while busy gathering apples in the highest tree,
he saw the wolf approaching.
"Do try one of these," he called down,
throwing an apple as far as he could.
When the wolf chased after the apple, the little pig
shimmied down the tree and made it safely home.

The next day the wolf came again.

Really he was *quite* put out.

"There's a fair today on Hog Hill," he said.

"Would you care to go?"

"Why don't we meet there?" said the little pig.

"Would three o'clock suit you?"

"Colossal," said the wolf.

"Three it is."

(Just to make sure, *he* would be there at two.)

At one in the afternoon the little pig
went to the fair and had a fine time—
so fine that he lost track of the hour.
Suddenly out of the corner of his eye
he saw the wolf coming up the hill.
Without a minute to spare, the little pig
jumped inside an empty butter churn
and rolled down the hill toward the wolf.

Well, the wolf was so scared,
he ran all the way home.

That evening the wolf went to the little pig's house
and told him how frightened he'd been
by a great round thing that came down the hill.
"Frightened you, did I?" said the little pig.
"That great round thing was a butter churn,
and I was inside!"
This was simply too much for the wolf to stand.
"I've been nice long enough!" he cried.
"I'm going to eat you up right now!"
And he climbed onto the roof.
When the little pig saw this, he put a big iron pot
in the fireplace and quickly stoked the fire.

"Here I come!"
cried the wolf.
"Dinnertime!"

"You can say that again!" said the little pig.
And he cooked the mean old wolf

and gobbled him up.